To my family . . . and those adjacent—I. V.

2024 First US edition
Translation copyright © 2024 by Charlesbridge; translated by Luisana Duarte Armendáriz
Illustrations copyright © 2022 by Verònica Aranda
All rights reserved, including the right of reproduction in whole or in part in any form. Charlesbridge and colophon are registered trademarks of Charlesbridge Publishing, Inc.
At the time of publication, all URLs printed in this book were accurate and active. Charlesbridge, the translator, the author, and the illustrator are not responsible for the content or accessibility of any website.

Published by Charlesbridge
9 Galen Street
Watertown, MA 02472
(617) 926-0329
www.charlesbridge.com

Una carta © First published by Edicions Bromera, 2022 (www.bromera.com)
© Text by Irene Verdú, 2022
© Illustrations by Verònica Aranda, 2022

institut ramon llull Illustrations in this US work supported by Institut Ramon Llull.

Library of Congress Cataloging-in-Publication Data
Names: Verdú, Irene, 1973– author. | Aranda, Verònica, illustrator. | Duarte Armendáriz, Luisana, translator.
Title: The letter / Irene Verdu; illustrated by Verònica Aranda; translated by Luisana Duarte Armendáriz.
Other titles: Carta. English
Description: First US edition. | Watertown, MA: Charlesbridge, 2024. | Originally published in Spanish as: Una carta. Alzira [Spain]: Algar, ©2022. | Audience: Ages 3–7. | Audience: Grades K–1. | Summary: Grumpy Mr. Cat is touched by a letter that the wind blew into his house and tries to find out who sent it.
Identifiers: LCCN 2023030509 (print) | LCCN 2023030510 (ebook) | ISBN 9781623544812 (hardcover) | ISBN 9781632894243 (ebook)
Subjects: LCSH: Letters—Juvenile fiction. | Cats—Juvenile fiction. | Animals—Juvenile fiction. | Friendship—Juvenile fiction. | CYAC: Letters—Fiction. | Cats—Fiction. | Animals—Fiction. | Friendship—Fiction. | LCGFT: Picture books.
Classification: LCC PZ7.1.V4618 Le 2024 (print) | LCC PZ7.1.V4618 (ebook) | DDC 863.92 [Fic]—dc23/eng/20230811
LC record available at https://lccn.loc.gov/2023030509
LC ebook record available at https://lccn.loc.gov/2023030510

Illustrations done digitally in Photoshop
Display type set in Canvas Script by Ryan Martinson
Text type set in Digby by Amy Dietrich
Handlettering by Ellie Erhart
Printed by 1010 Printing International Limited in Huizhou, Guangdong, China
Production supervision by Nicole Turner
Designed by Ellie Erhart

Printed in China
(hc) 10 9 8 7 6 5 4 3 2 1

This work received the Premio Algar de Album Illustrado (Algar Prize for Children's Literature) in Spain under its original title after its first publication. The panel was composed of Carol Borràs, Maria Bravo, Rosa Mengual, and Xelo Pérez.

The Letter

Irene Verdú

Illustrated by Verònica Aranda

Translated by Luisana Duarte Armendáriz

The mail carrier was surprised by a downpour and hurried. He lost the letter without noticing.
That day after the rain, the wind found the letter.

It was in a puddle. The water had erased the writing on the envelope, and it was impossible to know who had sent it or to whom it was addressed.

That's why the wind decided to open it and read it.

It was a lovely letter.
It simply said, *I love you.*

Since it was so beautiful, the wind thought it would be a shame if it didn't reach someone.

So the wind blew
and let the letter choose
its own destiny.
 The letter lifted up to the sky
and then fell from there.

The letter glided.

It reached Mr. Cat's roof, slid down his chimney, and landed on his head. At that moment he was sprawled in his favorite chair.

Mr. Cat was clean and orderly. He lived in a comfortable house that was perfect for friends to visit.

But Mr. Cat was a sourpuss. He didn't have a single friend, couldn't stand visits, and wouldn't even open the door for the mail carrier.

"Better a lonely cat than a disappointed one!" he muttered to himself whenever he felt sad, which was often.

But then Mr. Cat read the letter that had come down his chimney. He suddenly felt very happy.

Somebody loves me! he thought, rejoicing.

He wanted to investigate who had sent the mysterious letter. So without giving it another thought, he went out to search.

On the street he saw Ms. Goose. She was going to the farm carrying a very heavy basket.
Maybe she sent the letter! Mr. Cat thought.

He was excited. He hurried to offer his help, and he carried her basket the rest of the way.

Such kindness surprised Ms. Goose so much that she was almost speechless.

"Honk, honk," she nervously stammered.

And she left without even saying thank you.
   Mr. Cat felt disappointed.

Honk, honk!

But soon afterward he saw Mrs. Hen. She was trying to get one of her chicks down from the top of a tree.

Maybe she sent the letter! Mr. Cat thought.

He was excited. He hurried to offer his help, and he carefully brought the youngling down.

"Cluck, cluck!" The hen was so distracted by her chick's stunt that she took her baby by the wing and they both walked away without even thanking Mr. Cat.

Cluck, cluck!

Mr. Cat felt very disappointed.

But right then, Mr. Cat ran into Shepherd Dog. He was trying to jumpstart his old motorcycle without any success.

Maybe he sent the letter! Mr. Cat thought.

Vroom, vroom!

He was excited. He hurried to offer his help, and he pushed the old motorcycle until it started.

"Woof!" the dog barked. He happily drove away without even giving thanks to Mr. Cat.

Poor Mr. Cat. He was utterly let down. He thought about his old belief that being lonely was better than being disappointed.

He walked home very slowly.

When he finally reached his house, he couldn't believe what he saw.

Ms. Goose was waiting for him with a homemade cake.

Mrs. Hen and her chicks had a basket of fresh fruit.

And Shepherd Dog held a jug of tasty milk.

"This is all for you!" Ms. Goose said.

"For your kindness," Mrs. Hen said.

"We're sorry we didn't thank you right away," Shepherd Dog said.

For the first time, Mr. Cat knew what it felt like to be loved.

He opened the door to his house for his new friends.

You're probably wondering . . .
What about the letter?

The wind snuck in through the open door of Mr. Cat's house.
    It blew the letter and lifted it up to the sky once again.